Danebridge started th
fashion. They put tog
dangerous attacks, fo
goalkeeper to make t
second equalizer looked likely until a
Hanfield striker broke loose and sprinted clear of Andrew and the rest of the defence.

Chris came out to meet him but the attacker wasn't to be panicked into shooting wildly. He stayed calm and tried to dribble round the keeper. Chris lunged at the ball just as the boy whisked it away out of reach and then fell as Chris's arm caught his leg and brought him down.

'Penalty!'

Rob Childs is a Leicestershire teacher with many years' experience of coaching and organizing school and area representative sports teams. *The Big Prize* is one of a series of footballing titles about Andrew and Christopher Weston, two soccer-mad brothers.

Also available by Rob Childs,
for sports fans everywhere:

YOUNG CORGI BOOKS
THE BIG CHANCE
THE BIG DAY
THE BIG GAME
THE BIG GOAL
THE BIG KICK
THE BIG PRIZE
THE BIG STAR
THE BIG BREAK
THE BIG MATCH
THE BIG FREEZE

THE BIG FOOTBALL COLLECTION
– containing
THE BIG GAME
THE BIG MATCH
THE BIG PRIZE

CORGI YEARLING BOOKS
SANDFORD ON TOUR
SOCCER AT SANDFORD
ALL GOALIES ARE CRAZY
SOCCER MAD

ROB CHILDS

THE BIG PRIZE

Illustrated by Aidan Potts

YOUNG CORGI BOOKS

THE BIG PRIZE

A YOUNG CORGI BOOK : 0 552 52823 4

First publication in Great Britain

PRINTING HISTORY
Young Corgi edition published 1994
Reprinted 1995, 1996 (twice), 1997

This book [illegible] olbook by
[illegible]

Young Co[illegible] hers Ltd,
61–63 Uxbridge Road, Ealing, London W5 5SA,
in Australia by Transworld Publishers (Australia) Pty Ltd,
15–25 Helles Avenue, Moorebank, NSW 2170,
and in New Zealand by Transworld Publishers (NZ) Ltd,
3 William Pickering Drive, Albany, Auckland.

The Random House Group Limited supports The Forest Stewardship Council® (FSC®), the leading international forest-certification organisation. Our books carrying the FSC label are printed on FSC®-certified paper. FSC is the only forest-certification scheme supported by the leading environmental organisations, including Greenpeace. Our paper procurement policy can be found at
www.randomhouse.co.uk/environment

Printed and bound in Great Britain by Clays Ltd, St Ives plc

With thanks to Kyle and Dan, two real soccer mascots

1 Beat-the-Goalie

'Roll up! Roll up!' cried Andrew Weston at the top of his voice. 'Beat-the-Goalie! Score two out of three to win a prize. Roll up!'

'Wish you'd *belt* up,' muttered Chris, his younger brother. 'This isn't a fairground, you know.'

Andrew grinned. 'Got to attract people and earn some cash. Thought that's what we're here for.'

'It is. But just do it quieter, will you? I can't put up with you shouting your head off like that all afternoon.'

Andrew ignored him as usual. 'C'mon, folks, try your luck,' he called out. 'You don't need any skill – the goalie's rubbish!'

Chris threw a football at him, but his brother saw it coming and ducked. 'Missed!' Andrew laughed. 'But I won't. C'mon, I'll be your first

customer and show everybody how easy it is.'

'It'll cost you twenty pence,' Grandad chuckled from his seat nearby.

'What! You're going to charge *me*?'

'Course we are. All for a good cause, remember,' Grandad replied, casting a quick glance over the playing field. He could see there was already quite a crowd jostling around the jumble sale tables. 'Going to be a marvellous day – I can feel it in my old bones.'

Mr Jones, Danebridge Primary School's headmaster, was optimistic too. The February sun was shining kindly on their special Fun Day and he felt very proud of his pupils. The whole event had been their own idea in the first place and they had set up most of the stalls and games themselves.

The children were trying to raise money for extra sports kit and equipment. Not just for the benefit of the school, but also for a local charity which ran a sports club for disabled youngsters.

Matthew Clarke, in his final year at Danebridge, was one of the main organizers of the Fun Day. Mr Jones spotted him now making a bee-line for the Weston family's *Beat-the-Goalie* competition and smiled. He might have guessed it wouldn't take long before soccer-mad Matthew went to have a go at that.

Grandad saw him coming as well. 'Matthew knows what your shooting's like, Andrew,' he joked. 'He's coming to fetch the balls you smack over the bar!'

'No need for him to bother,' Andrew answered confidently. 'They're all gonna end up inside the net.'

'No chance!' Chris scoffed.

'Oh yeah?'

'Yeah!' Although he was two years younger, Chris tried to give back as good as he got. It didn't always work, especially if Andrew lost his temper, but he had learnt to stick up for himself.

Andrew gave him the kind of hard stare that Chris knew so well. This was serious stuff. Andrew meant business. His elder brother's pride was at stake and he carefully placed the ball for the first penalty a few metres in front of the small-sized goal.

Chris crouched on the line, the low crossbar only just above his head. He rubbed his gloved hands down his tracksuit bottoms and got ready to

spring either way as Andrew ran in to shoot.

The young goalie was already good enough to have played twice for Danebridge when the regular school team keeper had been out of action, so he wasn't easily fooled. But he was this time. Chris felt sure that Andrew would blast the ball. That was his big brother's usual penalty-taking method when they played together in the garden.

Chris threw himself to his right, but instead the ball skimmed along the ground into the opposite corner of the goal. Andrew had placed it perfectly with a gentle side-footer. He punched the air in triumph as though he'd scored the winning goal in the F.A. Cup Final.

'Well done, little brother, that was brill. Funniest thing I've seen in years.'

Chris pulled a face. 'You've not won yet. It's two out of three.'

'No trouble,' Andrew smirked, plonking the second ball on the penalty spot. 'So where's this one gonna go, eh?'

'Just shut up and hit it,' Chris replied. He decided to dive to his left, trying to outguess Andrew – but he was wrong again. His heart sank as the ball flashed the other way and then he heard a clunk and Andrew's groan. The shot had clipped the outside of the post and gone wide of the target.

'How lucky can you get?' cried Andrew.

'Must be those lucky gloves of his,' Matthew called out.

'*Lucky* gloves!' Andrew snorted. 'They're just a tatty old pair that should have gone to a jumble sale ages ago.'

'They're witch's gloves,' Chris claimed.

'Rubbish! They belonged to old Mrs Witchell next door, that's all. She's no more a witch than I am.'

Chris shrugged. 'Well, I like to think they've got a magic spell on them. They haven't let me down yet.'

'There's always a first time. You won't even smell this next one.'

Andrew was bored with little side-footers. This was going to be a master-blaster and he took an extra long run-up.

This could go anywhere, Chris said

to himself. Might as well just stay where I am and see what happens.

He did, standing upright in the centre of the goal as Andrew struck the penalty. It sped straight at him like a cannonball, the force of it almost knocking Chris off his feet. He could only parry the ball in self-defence, protecting his face, but it was enough to stop the shot going in.

Andrew lashed the rebound into the net in fury but he knew that it didn't count. There were no second chances in this competition.

Grandad quickly calmed Andrew down. 'Doesn't matter, forget it – everybody's a winner today, especially the charity. Young Chris here will

take some beating in these small goals.'

Andrew nodded and then flashed a grin at his brother. 'I'll have another go at you later,' he promised.

'Fine, and I'll try my luck with you when it's your turn in goal,' Chris replied. 'I've got a feeling this is going to be my lucky day!'

2 *Egg-cellent!*

'Can I have a go now?'

'Sure thing, Matthew,' Chris said. 'As long as you've got twenty pence.'

Matthew Clarke grinned, flipped a coin into the tin and rolled his wheel-chair into position. He put the brake on to hold it steady. 'As I can't kick, I'm going to head the balls past you instead.'

'Come in a bit closer, then,' Chris told him. 'The penalty spot's too far away for headers.'

'I'm OK from here. I've been practising.'

Chris never doubted it. They often played together and he knew how keen Matthew was to do well at games. Sometimes Matthew would end up toppling out of the chair in his eagerness to reach the ball first.

Matthew leant back in his seat, took a deep breath and tossed the football up in front of him. The top half of his body then suddenly snapped forward like the spring on a mousetrap. His legs may have been weak but his neck muscles were powerful enough. They sent the ball hurtling from his forehead towards the target.

'Great goal!' cried Andrew from behind the net. 'Right in the top corner.'

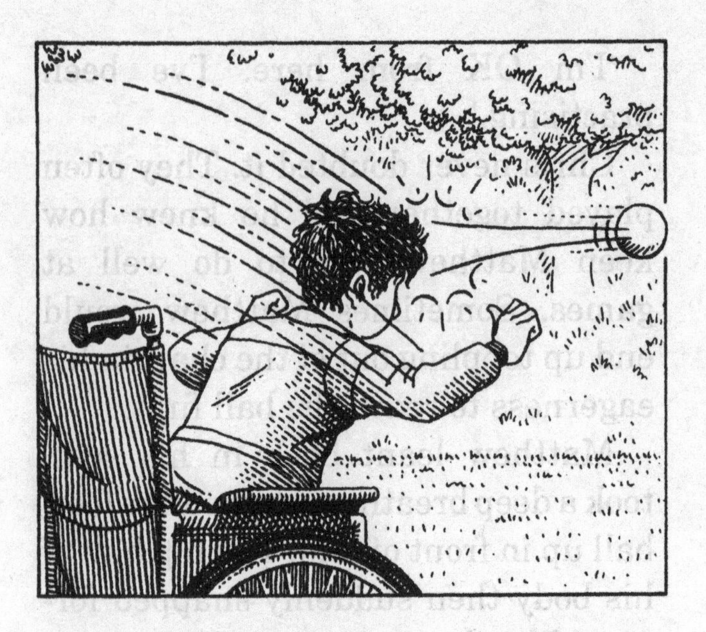

Chris had dived full length but had still been caught out by the speed and accuracy of the header. He missed the next one, too, as Matthew twisted his head round at the last moment and sent the goalkeeper the wrong way.

Andrew was doubled up with laughter. 'Come on, Matt's won already. I'll go in goal for his last effort. Give him a proper contest!'

Chris shrugged and swapped places, exchanging a quick wink with his friend. 'Show him how it's done, Matthew,' he urged.

This time Matthew's body barely moved, but his head suddenly whipped forward with an explosive grunt and the ball flew to the keeper's left. Andrew got a hand to it but could only help the ball into the net.

'Incredible, Matt!' Andrew gasped. 'Had no idea you could head a ball like that. You're better than anybody in our school team.'

Matthew's face was a picture of delight at such praise. 'You ought to see me play wheelchair soccer in the gym with the other disabled kids,' he said. 'I'm the leading scorer.'

'I bet you are,' Andrew laughed. 'I wouldn't like to have to mark you.'

'I'd run you over if you got in my

way,' Matthew grinned. 'I play rough. I'm always damaging my chair.'

As Matthew tore open the wrapping of his chocolate bar prize, more of the boys from the charity's sports club came over to join in. They attended various schools in and around the nearby town of Selworth, but this afternoon they were all the special guests of Danebridge. Between them, they kept the brothers busy for the next hour. Some were able to kick the ball quite well, a few threw it and others used their head like Matthew to try and score. One even used his crutches.

Chris was in goal most of the time and allowed everyone to gain some success against him. If they missed

with both their first two goes, Chris made sure, somehow, that the third went it. His comical 'slips' added to the fun and nobody minded that he wasn't always trying too hard to make a save.

Chris carried on the same way all afternoon. He let little children stand right up to the goal so they could score at least once, but he threw himself about everywhere to stop the shots of people his own age and much older.

Grandad almost purred with pleasure at some of his grandson's saves. Chris was in great form and his performance didn't go unnoticed by others too. Mr Jones, for example. The headmaster knew how much Christopher Weston loved goalkeeping, but it was the boy's sportsmanship that impressed him even more.

All the activities stopped briefly while the main raffle was drawn.

'Green ticket, number twenty-six!' announced Mr Jones loudly. 'A bit early yet for Easter, but our next prize is a giant chocolate egg!'

Chris could hardly believe his eyes. There in his muddy glove lay that very ticket. 'That's me!' he squeaked, his voice cracking in excitement. 'I've won!'

As Chris ran forward to receive the boxed egg, Andrew muttered to one of his pals, 'Typical of our kid's luck, that is, Duggie. He just buys one ticket, and here's me with a fistful and bet I get nothing!'

John Duggan laughed. 'Never mind

the Easter Egg. We're after the star prize today, aren't we?'

'What? In the raffle?'

'Nah!' Duggie sneered. 'You know . . .'

'Oh, yeah, that. Right!' Andrew caught on to what Duggie meant and stared at the man helping the headmaster with the draw. He was Martin North, team captain of Selworth Town Football Club.

The Town had agreed to sponsor the Day's events and several first team players had come along to join in the fun. They had also promised a very special prize of their own.

The players were going to choose one of the pupils to be Selworth's mascot for their next home game in the famous F.A. Cup competition. And that lucky person would have the honour of running out in front of the team, wearing a free souvenir kit in the Club's colours.

Duggie, like the rest of the Danebridge soccer squad, was desperate to catch their eye. 'North's already seen me doing a bit of ball juggling,' he boasted. 'Said I was good, too. Must be in with a chance of being picked.'

'Sorry! He'll forget all about you when he gets over to our game and sees me in action,' Andrew taunted him.

Chris, too, had dreamt of being chosen as mascot. But for the moment at least, he was more than happy with his huge Easter Egg. He put it in the corner of the net for safe-keeping.

And he would soon need to be a safe keeper to protect it – Martin North and Dave Adams, Selworth's top goalscorer and chief penalty-taker, were heading their way!

The brothers saw them early, still surrounded by a pack of autograph hunters, but not as early as Duggie.

'C'mon, little Westy,' he called out. 'My turn. I'm gonna show you – and them – how penalties should be taken.'

Chris sighed. Duggie could be such a big-head at times. He always wanted to prove how good he was at scoring goals and loved nothing better than hammering the ball past him into the net.

Chris braced himself as the striker ran in but barely had time to move. The ball smashed against the cross-bar and spun up into the air before he could even blink.

Duggie threw his hands up in horror, but struck the next one just as hard. He managed to keep this one low but it was too near the goalie. The ball rebounded off Chris's knee to safety, the force of it making him hobble around for a few moments as he rubbed the sore spot.

'The talent-spotters won't think much of that effort, Duggie!' Andrew chortled. 'Last go coming up.'

Frustrated, Duggie charged in again and Chris this time decided to dive out of the way of the missile. But as he did, there was a sickening crunch behind him. He had forgotten about the egg! The ball had scored a direct hit on the box, buckling it up and bursting the packaging.

Everyone gathered round to inspect the damage, hushed at first until they sensed that Chris saw the funny side of it too. Then the jokes came.

'An *egg-cellent* shot, Duggie, my old mate!' whooped Andrew.

'Yeah, thanks to my *egg-stra* power!' cackled Duggie.

Generously, Chris began to share out the broken pieces of chocolate. 'Might as well eat it all now, I guess,' he smiled.

'Good old Duggie!' laughed Matthew. 'Couldn't have aimed it better myself. A fine *egg-sample* of penalty-taking!'

3 *Star Prize*

When the two Selworth Town players finally arrived on the scene, it wasn't just shyness that prevented the boys from speaking at first. Their mouths were still full of chocolate.

Chris at last found his voice. 'Er, sorry, we don't seem to have any Easter Egg left to offer you. It's all gone.'

The men laughed. 'So we see,' said Martin North. 'Not to worry. Dave here wants to try and win a bar of

chocolate instead for himself. You the keeper?'

Chris nodded, hardly able to believe he was about to face Dave Adams, Selworth's star striker.

'Right, then, in goal and let's see if Dave can put any past you.'

Quite a crowd gathered round to watch the big shoot-out, the other lads full of envy. They would have given anything to be in Chris's boots right now. Or even in his 'lucky' gloves . . .

He was beaten for pace by Adams's first penalty but the ball struck the inside of the post. It flew across the goal-line, hit the other post and bounced straight back into Chris's waiting arms. He stood there hugging the ball and grinning like a chimp at a tea-party.

Adams tried again, but Chris this time didn't need any help from the woodwork. He pulled off a wonder-save, finger-tipping the ball just over the bar to earn even louder cheers than before.

The Selworth winger shook his head in amazement. 'I just can't beat this guy!' Adams cried out, attempting to cover his embarrassment with a laugh. 'Sign him up, somebody – he can come and play for us!'

'One left, Dave,' the captain reminded his teammate jokily. 'Miss this and you won't be able to show your face in the dressing-room again. We'll have to sell you!'

He did miss it. He took extra careful aim because of the small-sized goal

and was clever enough to send the boy the wrong way. But Chris still managed to block the shot with his outstretched leg and keep it out.

'Fantastic!' Matthew yelled as Chris found himself mobbed. 'You're a real star now!'

Andrew leant on the goalpost, jealous of Chris's sudden new fame. The way Andrew had pictured it, this sort of thing was supposed to be happening to him, not his kid brother.

The Selworth captain now had to step forward to save the Club's reputation and Chris's luck didn't quite last out. North scored twice, but not before Chris had pushed his first effort against the post.

The Fun Day proved a great success, raising more money for the school and the charity than they had ever expected. Right at the end, after presenting a cheque from Selworth Town F.C., North announced their decision.

'We've seen some very promising sporting talent here this afternoon, but one boy for us has really stood out. Not even our best penalty-taker could beat him.'

The player paused as everyone looked round at a red-faced Chris. 'And with his kind of luck,' North continued, 'winning that Easter Egg too, he's got to be our choice for team mascot in the F.A. Cup.'

Chris was pushed up to the front through the crowd to shake Martin North's hand. 'Here he is,' the captain greeted him. 'A big round of applause,

please, for Christopher Weston, a very *egg-cited* young man!'

Danebridge School had a cup-tie of their own first, a quarter-final match away from home. Chris went to watch Andrew play as usual and invited Matthew to come, too, his wheelchair folded and strapped to the roof-rack of Grandad's car.

Matthew tried to support the school team as often as he could, cheering himself silly from his chair. As far as he was concerned, it was the next best thing to being out on the pitch, running around with his pals.

He knew he would never be able to do that. But thanks to the fund-raising, the charity could now start to provide more chances for him and others like him to enjoy their various wheelchair sports such as soccer and basketball.

As Chris pushed him along towards the touchline, Matthew said, 'You ought to be playing today, after what you did in goal on the Fun Day.'

'Simon Garner's still first choice,' Chris replied. 'He's older.'

'Not better, though.'

'Well, thanks, but Simon's a pretty good keeper really.'

Matthew giggled. 'He's not as good as you at saving penalties!'

'Let's just hope he doesn't have to face any today, then,' Chris said as the two teams jogged out on to the pitch.

Tim Lawrence, the Danebridge skipper, won the toss and decided to kick first into the strong breeze.

'Tim always prefers to have the wind behind him in the second half when everyone's a bit tired,' Matthew explained. 'But if it was me, I'd use the wind straightaway.'

'Why's that?' asked Chris.

'Try to go a few goals up early on and hope the other lot give in.'

Chris nodded. 'What do you think, Grandad?'

'Makes sense,' he agreed, struggling to light his pipe in the wind. 'There was one game I played as a kid – howling gale, it was. So strong, we could hardly get the ball out of our own penalty area. Six–nil down at half-time, we were, but reckoned we'd get our own back in the second half.'

'What happened?'

'Ended up losing ten–nil,' Grandad chuckled. 'Pesky wind went and died

down all of a sudden when we changed round, just like somebody had gone and switched it off!'

'How do you remember the score after all this time?' Matthew asked.

Grandad gave Chris a wink. His grandson already knew the answer. 'I was in goal, lad, that's why. Only time in my life I let in double figures! Goalies always remember bad days like that.'

4 *One of Those Days*

There was no danger this game of Simon Garner suffering the same fate as Grandad.

Although Danebridge were forced to defend for much of the first half, Simon had not been especially busy. Andrew at centre-back had the defence well organized. Most of the home side's attacks broke down before getting a clear sight of goal.

Then, on a rare raid, Duggie raced away to shoot Danebridge ahead and they looked well set up for an easy win in the second half. But by the time the referee blew for the interval, they were 2–1 down instead. Both goals came in the space of three minutes.

The equalizer was a disaster. Andrew was certain the attacker was offside, but even so, his shot was a tame one. Simon seemed to have it well covered until somehow he let the ball squirm from his grasp and slip over the line.

Simon's error gave him the jitters. He soon fumbled another shot and Andrew had to hook the ball out of play. It only delayed the second goal briefly. The nervous keeper couldn't hold the corner and saw the ball lashed back past him into the roof of the net.

'Sorry!' Simon apologized to his teammates as they gathered round Mr Jones at the interval.

'Forget about it, Simon,' the headmaster said. 'Everybody makes mistakes. I don't expect you to have much to do now with the wind in our favour. Let's work hard, lads, to keep the ball in their half.'

They did just that. Simon was little more than a spectator and watched his team first draw level and then go in front. In the end, to his great relief, Danebridge ran up a 4–2 lead which was enough to see them safely through to the semi-finals.

'I could have played in goal second half and it wouldn't have made any difference,' Matthew joked as he and Chris waited for the teams to change afterwards.

Chris was tossing a ball to him to

head back when the headmaster came out of the school building and saw them. 'Enjoy the match, lads?'

They nodded and Mr Jones then spoke directly to Chris. 'Fancy a bit of a game yourself next week, do you?'

Chris jumped at the chance to play for the school again.

'Good,' said Mr Jones. 'Knew you'd be pleased. I'd like to give you some more experience and it'll help to keep Simon on his toes, knowing you're around. I'll give you half a game each.'

As the headmaster went off, Matthew said, 'Lucky old you. You know what that game is, don't you?'

Chris shook his head.

'It's a vital league match. Bet he's hoping that some of your luck will rub off on the team. We'll need it, too. We're playing Hanfield and they're top of the league.'

Grandad butted in. 'It's also the same day, remember, when you're due to be Selworth's mascot.'

'Wow!' Matthew whistled. 'Playing in the morning, mascot in the afternoon. What a day! Hope those gloves of yours keep working their magic!'

'Can't wait till this afternoon!'

The week had dragged by so slowly for Chris. His mind kept drifting away to the excitement that lay ahead, and he'd been told off in class many times for day-dreaming. 'Just think,' he babbled on. 'Little me trotting out with the Selworth team in front of all those people!'

He was trying to keep up with his older brother as they jogged towards the village recreation ground for the school's league match.

Suddenly Andrew stopped and turned on him. 'Look, you've been going on all week about not being able to wait till Saturday. Now it's here, you start on about this afternoon. We've got a big game ourselves this morning first, never mind Selworth.'

'I know, I know,' Chris replied. 'But hardly the F.A. Cup, is it?'

'So? It's just as important to us. We've got to beat Hanfield to stand any chance of winning the league championship.'

'I'll be doing my best, don't worry.'

'Just see that you do,' Andrew said gruffly. 'We can't afford to have any slip-ups today.'

Sadly, however, when Chris made his promised appearance after half-time, Danebridge were already trailing 2–1, just as in the previous game. And once again, Simon had not had the happiest of times. After Tim had equalized Hanfield's early opening goal, Simon was slow to get down to a low skimming shot and let the ball bobble under his body.

The goalkeeper hung his head in dismay, not wanting to catch anybody's eye. The kind of form he was in, he would probably have dropped it anyway!

Watching from the garden wall of his cottage next to the recky pitch, Grandad gave Chris the thumbs-up sign. Chris returned it and tugged nervously on his 'lucky' gloves. He so much wanted to do well. A good performance today and he might even keep Simon out of the team. Thoughts about his mascot duties somehow had to be forgotten, at least for the moment.

Despite being behind, Danebridge started the half in bright fashion. They put together a couple of dangerous attacks, forcing the other goalkeeper to make two good saves. A second equalizer looked likely until a Hanfield striker broke loose and sprinted clear of Andrew and the rest of the defence.

Chris came out to meet him but the attacker wasn't to be panicked into shooting wildly. He stayed calm and tried to dribble round the keeper. Chris lunged at the ball just as the boy whisked it away out of reach and then fell as Chris's arm caught his leg and brought him down.

'Penalty!' screamed all the

Hanfield team and supporters. Mr Jones, the referee, reluctantly had to agree.

'You great wally!' cried Andrew, standing over his brother. 'What did you go and do a clumsy thing like that for?'

'I didn't mean to,' Chris defended himself. 'It just happened.'

'There was no need to charge out of goal like that. I'd have caught him up before he shot.'

Chris knew that wasn't true but had no chance to argue.

'Don't get at each other, you two,' Mr Jones ordered. 'That doesn't help matters at all.'

Andrew still had the last word. 'Right, little brother, if you're so brilliant at saving penalties, make up for it by stopping this one.'

'C'mon, Chris,' Matthew shouted from the touchline. 'You show 'em. Remember Dave Adams!'

Chris frowned. This, he knew, was a completely different situation. For a start, the recky goal was huge, and this was for real, not for a bit of fun.

Waiting on the goal-line, Chris watched the penalty-taker run in. The boy tried to disguise which way he was going to place the kick, but Chris guessed correctly. He threw himself to the right but the ball was well struck – hard and high. Chris felt it brush past his fingers and then heard the sound that all goalkeepers dread and all goalscorers love. The

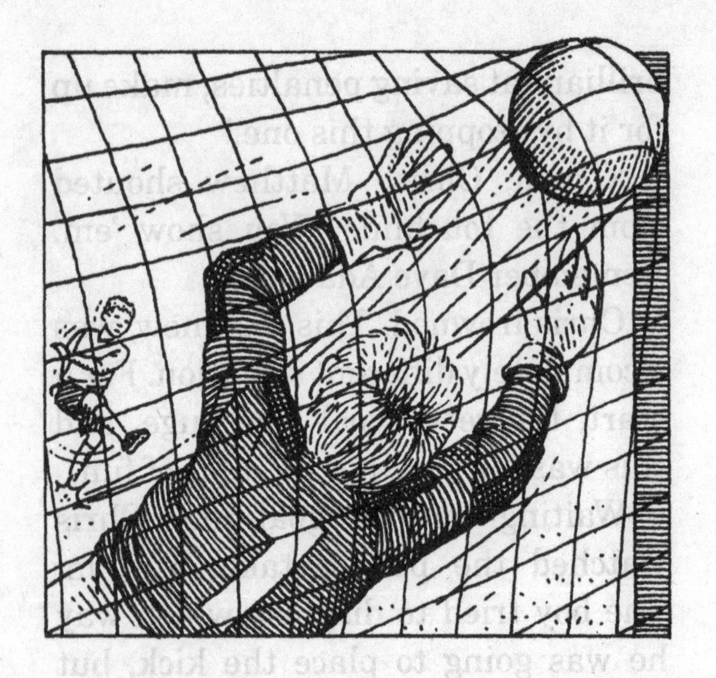

swish of the football hitting the back of the netting.

Danebridge were now 3–1 behind and their dreams of the league title were disappearing fast in the cold light of day.

Duggie, for one, was not about to give up, however. He soon shocked the league leaders with a superb headed goal from a corner and sent another shot only a fraction wide.

But the brave fightback was halted in its tracks. Chris blocked one effort during a goalmouth scramble, and was unable to keep hold of the ball again when it was driven at him through a crowd of bodies. It popped out of his gloves and a Hanfield player finally forced it over the line to put them two goals ahead once more.

Duggie fished the ball out the net and couldn't resist a dig at the miserable young goalkeeper before he hurried back upfield to kick off. 'Huh! Some *lucky* mascot you're gonna be – Selworth have got no chance this afternoon with *you* around!'

5 *Lucky Mascot?*

Duggie's taunt stung Chris. He ripped off his 'lucky' witch's gloves and threw them into the back of the net.

'Never going to wear those useless things again. They don't give me enough grip. Wish I'd worn my proper goalie gloves.'

Andrew was unsympathetic. 'We've got no chance now, thanks to you.'

'That's not fair. You were losing even before I came on.'

'Yeah, and you've gone and made it worse.'

'Anybody can have an off day,' muttered Chris.

'True,' Andrew sneered, 'but why did you choose this one?'

Chris pulled a face. The special day had not started quite the way he'd hoped. At this rate, his teammates would probably jeer rather than cheer him when he took the field with Selworth that afternoon.

Hanfield played with more and more confidence now with a cushion of a two-goal lead and set about increasing it further. Not even Tim and Duggie could work any miracles to get Danebridge back into the game.

Chris was kept too busy to worry any more about his earlier errors. He began to show his true abilities, catching the ball cleanly with his bare hands and making two outstanding saves. But all in vain. The damage had already been done – at least in terms of dashing the school's hopes of winning the league title.

For Chris, unfortunately, the real damage was still to come. As the game entered the last minute, Hanfield mounted yet another attack.

The ball was swept across into the goalmouth, Andrew headed it away, but straight to a player lurking outside the area. He hammered it back in on the volley beautifully. Chris made a move for the ball, but then saw it take a massive deflection off a Danebridge leg. He had to twist back suddenly in the opposite direction.

'Ow!' His ankle gave way underneath him and he yelped in pain. He sank to the ground as the ball looped into the net for Hanfield's fifth goal but Chris was past caring. His ankle felt like it was on fire.

Helping hands tried to lift him up. 'It's almost the end, Chris,' said Mr Jones. 'Can you carry on?'

The boy shook his head, forcing back the tears. He couldn't even stand up by himself. Then he heard

Grandad's voice. He hadn't seen that Grandad was already at his side.

Forgetting his age, Grandad had run across the pitch as soon as he realized that Chris was hurt. 'C'mon, my lad. Game's over for you. You're back to the cottage with me for some first aid. Bring his gear with you later, Andrew.'

Another spectator helped carry Chris off and into Grandad's kitchen while Andrew himself pulled on the green goalie top. When he reported back to the cottage after the match, joking that he'd kept a clean sheet, he found Chris with his foot wrapped up in a cold, wet towel.

'What's that for?' asked Andrew.

'Grandad's trying to prevent too

much swelling,' Chris said, wincing as Andrew bent to touch his ankle. 'Don't do that. I've twisted it.'

'Tough luck, our kid,' Andrew said, attempting to keep a straight face. 'What about this afternoon, then?'

Chris sighed heavily and shook his head. 'Dunno yet. Don't see how I can make it now I've done this. Can't really go crawling out in front of the team on my hands and knees, can I?'

Andrew smirked. 'I could always take your place.'

'Oh, yeah, you'd like that, wouldn't you? Leave me here suffering while you go off and hog all the glory for yourself.'

Andrew shrugged. 'Just a thought. Somebody's got to go and do it. Can't leave the Town without a mascot for their big cup match.'

That same terrible thought had been occupying Chris's mind ever since his injury. 'Looks like it's not going to be my day after all,' he groaned. 'Sorry about the goals I let in.'

Andrew shrugged. 'Doubt if we'd have beaten them anyway. Have to admit, they were a bit too good for us.'

There was a knock at Grandad's front door and in rolled Matthew in his wheelchair. 'Couldn't reach up to the bell,' he grinned. 'Thought I'd better come and see if I could do anything to help.'

By school minibus and cars, the Danebridge soccer squad arrived at Selworth stadium's main car-park in good time before the match. The Club

had given them all free grandstand tickets and the treat helped to make up for their own disappointment earlier.

Grandad took Matthew's wheelchair down from the roof-rack and Andrew began to help its user from the back seat of the car.

'I can manage. I'm not completely helpless, you know.'

Andrew laughed. 'OK, I'll just stand here and watch you struggle.'

Feeling everybody was watching him, the invalid hopped clumsily across the small gap and slumped into the chair. 'Made it, you see.'

'Sure! I can just see you trying to hop about all over the pitch!'

Chris smiled at the thought and gave up. 'OK, you win, I do need some help. Give me a push. I haven't got the hang of this thing yet.'

'Nor these!' added Grandad, tucking a pair of crutches under his arm. 'But you're going to need them in a bit, if you're wanting to go and meet the players down in the dressing-room.'

'Yeah!' Andrew agreed. 'No way am I going to lug you up and down any steps in Matt's wheelchair.'

Matthew Clarke had come to Chris's rescue. He would be at the match himself as usual, sitting in the area reserved for disabled spectators, but had offered to lend Chris his crutches and spare wheelchair.

Chris hadn't really fancied the idea, but Grandad and Andrew talked him into trying it. 'It's the only way you'll manage this afternoon with that bad ankle of yours,' Grandad told him. 'You've got to keep your weight off it for a while.'

'I'll feel stupid,' said Chris.

'You *are* stupid, getting yourself injured on a day like this,' Andrew replied. 'But it's either the chair or me taking your place. Take your pick!'

The wheelchair won but Andrew got his wish too. He was planning to

push Chris out on to the pitch himself!

'This has got to be some kind of joke!' Dave Adams cried when Chris wobbled into the dressing-room, his ankle heavily strapped up with bandages. 'I've been telling everyone that this kid who saved all my penalties was dead lucky – and then he goes and turns up on crutches!'

The players laughed at their teammate and listened with amusement as Grandad told them Chris's tale of woe.

'Great omen for the match, this is, lads, eh?' smiled the captain, giving Chris a wink. 'Even our lucky mascot's gone lame!'

6 *Catch!*

The roar from the packed crowd was deafening. As soon as the home team were spotted coming out of the players' tunnel, the chants and the cheers trebled in volume.

Then, for a moment, the sound died as the spectators looked more closely. Leading Selworth out on to the pitch was a lad in a wheelchair, kitted out as a goalkeeper and pushed by an older boy wearing a tracksuit. It wasn't exactly the sight they had been expecting!

The brothers were stunned by the noise. 'This is amazing!' cried Andrew, slapping Chris on his shoulder. 'Fantastic feeling!'

Chris could hardly hear him, but he was just as excited. He completely forgot about his nervousness and embarrassment in the thrill of the moment. He would dearly have loved to run out with the team properly, but at least being pushed was the next best thing.

As the players began to warm up at their favourite end of the ground in front of their fans, Andrew wheeled Chris towards the penalty area. Chris had promised to look out for Matthew near the corner flag and now saw him waving madly.

Chris had a bit of trouble waving back as he was trying to balance the crutches across the arms of the chair as well. He told Andrew to stop. 'Put the brake on. This is where I get off,' he shouted.

If anything, the crowd's cheers seemed to become even louder as Andrew helped his brother to stand up on the crutches and totter towards the goal. They were clearly enjoying the boy's spirited efforts to join in. Chris bashed at the ball with one of his crutches, and then with Andrew holding on to him, he unwisely attempted to kick at goal.

'Not with your bad foot,' Andrew reminded him.

His left ankle was still too sore

S.T.F.C

to put on the ground. Chris tried to balance briefly on the crutches and swing his right boot at the ball. He made contact, but lost his balance altogether and fell down in an untidy heap to hoots of laughter from the crowd.

Chris no longer minded. He was enjoying himself, too, being at the centre of all the fuss and attention. The Selworth goalkeeper helped Andrew lift the mascot back into the wheelchair.

'Safest place for you, I reckon,' the man grinned. 'You'll only make the injury worse fooling about on it. You sit there and I'll lob a few balls at you to catch, OK?'

'Great!' Chris cried. He didn't drop a single ball and received a loud cheer for every catch.

Andrew, meanwhile, cheekily took

the chance to whack a loose football into the unguarded net. 'What a goal!' he shouted and then realized the captains were being called to the centre-circle to toss up.

He ran back to the wheelchair. 'C'mon, you're needed,' he cried. 'Cor! This is getting hard work, pushing you. Why won't this thing go? Is it stuck in the mud or something?'

'It helps if you take the brake off first,' Chris suggested.

Andrew stood to one side to let Chris have the honour by himself of shaking hands with both captains and the referee. After the toss, Chris was given the coin as a souvenir and he posed for the press photographer with the players – and Andrew, too, when Martin North invited him to join the group.

Then, far too quickly, it was all over. The match was about to kick off and the mascot's brief moments in the limelight were at an end.

'Time to clear off,' Andrew said as he wheeled Chris back towards the touchline. 'Duty done – now the real business is about to start.'

'I'm still their mascot,' Chris protested. 'I've still got to try and bring them good luck.'

'I think you used up all your luck at the Fun Day,' Andrew replied.

The Club had found places near the trainers' benches beside the pitch for Grandad and the brothers. It was too difficult for Chris to reach the rest of the Danebridge party up in the stands.

'Magic! Right up close to the action,' Chris called out above the noise as the cup-tie got under way. 'I'm still lucky, you see, Andrew, getting us front row seats like this.'

Andrew grinned. 'Feels like we're almost playing. Might even have a kick or two if the ball comes out of play near us.'

Much to Andrew's regret, the ball never did come their way until near the end. By which time, the game was locked in stalemate and seemed set to be a goal-less draw.

A replay at home was obviously what the visiting team were hoping for. And they looked like achieving it, too, until Selworth's lucky mascot played a hand. Both hands, in fact.

The visitors were being jeered for their time-wasting tactics when, once again, the ball was booted aimlessly out of play for a throw-in.

As it flew over his head, Chris's natural goalkeeping instincts took over. He forgot all about his bad ankle. He leapt up from his seat to pluck the ball cleanly out of the air before it disappeared into the crowd behind him.

North charged up, demanding the ball, and Chris swiftly tossed it to him. Selworth's opponents had briefly relaxed when the ball went out and the quick throw-in caught them off guard.

The captain's accurate throw found Dave Adams unmarked and the star striker raced clear for goal. Adams

STFC

made no mistake. He drew the goal-keeper out, nipped skilfully round him and slotted the ball into the empty net. The crowd went wild with excitement.

'The winner!' screamed Andrew. 'Got to be!'

The Selworth players felt sure too. Many of them rushed across to Chris as part of their celebrations to ruffle his mop of fair hair.

'Great stuff, kid!' cried Adams. 'Told 'em you were lucky!'

After the referee blew the final whistle, Martin North came over to slap Chris on the back. 'We're through to the next round, thanks to you. We'd never have scored if you hadn't made that brilliant catch.'

Grandad chuckled with pride. 'He might only have one leg to stand on right now, but all a good keeper needs is two safe hands!'

'And a bit of luck,' Chris added happily.

'Aye, that helps, too,' Grandad smiled. 'But good players always make their own luck, m'boy, and don't you ever forget it!'

THE END

THE BIG DAY

Rob Childs

'We're going to win the cup!'

Danebridge School football team are through to the Cup Final and Andrew Weston, who plays in a key position in defence, can hardly wait for the big day. It's going to be the most important match of the whole year. His younger brother, Chris, is in on the action too, picked to be the team's substitute goalkeeper.

But the Weston brothers suddenly discover that they have a big problem. For the match clashes with an important family occasion – and their mother insists that they must drop out of the match. What can they do? They can't possibly miss the Final . . .

A tense and exciting football story – from kick-off to the final whistle.

0 552 52581 2